Sculptlings

The Professional Chickens

Sam the Policeman

Sculptlings ™ Stories written and illustrated
by Cynthia Lamb

Stories Edited by
Joshua Pilote and Dorothy Lawyer

Published by Sculptling Enterprises LLC.
Book design and cover design by Cynthia Lamb
Story edited by Joshua Pilote and Dorothy Lawyer

Publishers Note: This is a work of fiction. Names, characters and incidents are the author's imagination.

For written permission or for information about this title or to order other books and/or electronic media, contact the publisher:

Sculptling Enterprises LLC
cs@sculptlings.com

Library of Congress Control Number: 2022912784

ISBN 978-1-68531-069-1 (Soft Cover)
ISBN 978-1-68531-070-7 (Hard Cover)
ISBN 978-1-68531-071-4 (eBook)

Publisher's Cataloging In Publication Data
Sculptling Enterprises LLC
Wilton Manors FL
cs@sculptlings.com

Visit Sculptlings.com

Sculptlings books © are dedicated to my sister.
I could not have not made Sculptling Books happen
without your support.

The Professional Chickens was inspired by; Audrey Ballew.
Sam the Policeman was inspired by Mario Diaz.

A special thank you to Linda Fitzgerald, Joshua Pilote,
Dorothy Lawyer,Ezekiel Zambory and Ryan Zambory.

To Mario Diaz, thank you for all the loving support you gave me over the
years, you have helped me get to where I am today. The Sculptlings
Collection came to life with all my life lessons that you
supported me through. I am so thankful for your friendship.

Thank You all for your loving support.

Sam tries his best to help as much as he can.
He makes it his job, that's why he's a policeman.

Sam the policeman makes sure that
you are safe at night.

He walks the streets
and makes sure that people act right.

Sam makes it his job
to protect us all from danger.

That is why he tells us
not to talk to a stranger.

Sam spends his day reporting crimes
and finding leads.

He likes solving mysteries and doing good deeds.

He says, "It is important to help somebody in need."
"Because the more you give, the more that you receive."

A child wandered off and lost his way.
So Sam tried to find him that whole day.

Luckily Sam found him;
he just lost track of time.

Sam was glad he was okay,
and there was no actual crime.

Sometimes when people argue
they don't get along.

So Sam stands between them
so that nothing goes terribly wrong.

Sam steps in when he sees people fight.
He listens and decides who is right.

If you get in trouble for fighting,
Sam will put you in a cell.

He won't let you go until you say,
"I'm sorry, all is well."

Sam says, " Be good and do not lie, cheat or steal"
"If you break any laws, it will be a very big deal!"

Sam says, "When you do good things, people look up to you.

So be on your best behavior with everything you do.

When you do good things it fills you with pride.

You become a light when it is dark outside.

Sam says, "Let your light shine bright
for everyone to see.

Because by helping others
a good role model you will be.

SculpTlings Book Collection

Collect them all!

The Professional Chickens Series

Arthur the Farmer
Brad the Graduate
Byron the Fireman
Captain Corey and Catlin
Connor the Doctor
Laurence the Lawyer
Roger the Construction Worker
Sam the Policeman
Sherry the Chef
Violet the Pilot

The Musical Squirrel Series

Bo the Banjo Player
Chase the Bass Player
Gus the Guitarist
Jimmy the Drummer
Lee the Ukulele Player

The Sporty Little Penguins Series

Joe the Snowboarder
Patty the Paddleboarder
Peter the Skier
Porter the Longboarder
Shawn the Shortboarder
Slater the Skater

The Salty Sea Series

Jay the Salty Stingray
Octy the Salty Octopus
Scotty the Salty Sea Turtle

The Mischievous Mice Series

Freddy the Fruity Mouse
Kent the Manipulative Mouse
Pete the Sweet Mouse
Robby the Naughty Mouse

Meet The Author

Cynthia has always had a strong desire to help others. She has spent her life mentoring children and adults. "I believe in living by example and being a good role model". Cynthia loves helping kids with life's challenges and inspiring them to go after their dreams. She is highly motivated and enjoys seeing the results in the lives she touches.

Cynthia devoted 25 years of her life to developing the Sculptlings collection. Initially created as handmade ornaments, Sculptlings later evolved into these adorable story books. As a musician, she added music to her collection; now these characters have come to life, making you want to dance and sing along with them! Sculptlings are a result of Cynthia following her dreams, and she longs to encourage others to do the same. All of these characters have a special place in her heart--as each represents an experience in her life--and she hopes they will do the same for readers everywhere.

"The idea behind the books is to create an opportunity for conversations with kids. Sculptlings are easy to fall in love with, and the stories are entertaining for the whole family to enjoy."

Made in the USA
Las Vegas, NV
13 October 2022

57183173R00021